BATS!

Andrew Fusek Peters
and Alex McArdell

WAYLAND
www.waylandbooks.co.uk

Titles in the series

Bats!

978 0 7502 8231 4

Bullies and the Beast

978 0 7502 8229 1

Monster Savings

978 0 7502 8232 1

Poison!

978 0 7502 8230 7

CHAPTER 1

"Wow! That is one cool car!" I said to our PE teacher, Mr Price, in the school car park. I couldn't believe it. Last week, he was driving round in an old Micra. Now he had a shiny 4x4.

"She's a beauty, isn't she!" said Mr Price proudly. "My aunt died and she left me some cash. This beauty does 0 to 60 in under seven seconds!"

Then he frowned. "You should be changed, Kiran. You don't want to be late for football, do you?"

That was the thing about Price. If it was raining, he loved sending us out onto the pitch to get soaked. The wetter the better.

After we had dried out, there was a special assembly. The head teacher was telling us all about some new shopping centre that was going to be built next to the school grounds.

He told us that the builders would be bulldozing the local woods to make way for the new shops. It was progress, he said. The school would get a new extension as part of the deal.

The head invited Mr Price onto the stage.

"I am sure some of you know that there used to be long-eared bats in the barn deep in the woods," said Price. "As I am a bat expert, I was asked by the builders to check that all the bats had left."

He stopped speaking for a second
and I noticed his right leg twitching.

"And I can tell you that all the bats
have gone," he said. "Every last one
of them."

I was sure he was lying.

I saw Roz on the way out.

"That was so dull," she said. The hall was nearly empty, except for Jonesy, the old caretaker.

Jonesy's eyes sparked as he marched over to us, twirling his broom like a sword.

"I'll give you dull!" he said. "Those bats were lovely. It was magic to see them flying at dusk! And they were there last week. I saw them. Then yesterday they were gone. Just like that!"

Jonesy shook his head and shuffled away.

"I don't know," he muttered. "What's happening to the world?"

Roz looked at me.

"He's crazy!" she whispered.

"Maybe!" I replied. "But something is not right. I think we need to get Data Beast on the case!"

CHAPTER 2

Data Beast is our pet monster. He came out of Roz's computer. He seems to be made out of numbers and code. That's why we've called him Data Beast.

We were out walking in the local woods. Data Beast kept sniffing. "Smells... good!" he grunted.

"What's this?" said Roz. She pointed at the barbed wire fence across the path.

"Um, I think it's a fence!" I said.

"You annoy me sometimes," Roz snapped. "I meant the sign, you idiot!"

On the sign it said "Supersave - Shopping Heaven Here Soon!"

"The head teacher calls it progress," I said angrily. "That's a joke."

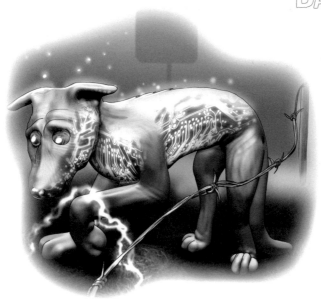

Just then Data Beast reached out and grabbed the barbed wire.

"Owwww!" he howled as black fluid leaked from his finger. "It hurt me."

"Losing the wood for a few stupid shops - that's going to hurt everyone," said Roz.

"Except for the people who make a lot of money out of it," I said.

Suddenly Data Beast said, "Little
one… scared… taken away!"

He pointed over the fence.

All I could see was the dim outline
of a barn.

"Data Beast is right. Look!" Roz whispered.

We both crouched down. There was a flickering light in one of the windows of the barn.

Then a figure came out of the barn. It was holding a box and looking left and right.

Data Beast was like a dog straining at the leash.

"Free the baby!" he groaned.

"Shhh, Data Beast. Wait!" Roz
muttered.

"What are you two doing?" said a
voice. We both turned to see a very
big security guard staring down at
us. I looked round for Data Beast. He
had vanished.

21

"There's someone in the barn!" said Roz. But when she looked back at the barn the shadowy figure had gone.

"Never mind about that," growled the security guard. "You're on private property. Scram before I call the police!"

CHAPTER 3

That evening, we were round at
Roz's house, mucking about on the
computer.

"I'm telling you, there was someone
in that barn," said Roz, "and Data
Beast sensed something bad was
happening."

Suddenly the computer screen exploded. Or rather, a stream of numbers burst out and formed itself into a monster-shaped lump of code. It was Data Beast!

"Please don't do that!" Roz squeaked.

"Sorry," said Data Beast. "Did not mean to scare."

"When that security guard spoke to us by the barn how did you vanish?" I asked Data Beast.

"I hid in phone, then flew by wi-fi to computer, where I... roost," he said.

"That's amazing," I said. "That's what birds do at night. They fly home to roost."

"Did you get to see inside the barn?" Roz asked.

Data Beast nodded.

"What did you see?" I asked.

"A baby," replied Data Beast. "Fur... wings... all alone... scared."

"A baby bat!" I said. "I knew there was something wrong. Someone is stealing the bats!"

Roz's mum put her head round the door. "I've made you some tea," she said. Then she turned to Data Beast.

"And I've got something special for you," she said. "It's an old motherboard they were throwing out at work. You get your teeth into that, my lovely!"

Roz's mum left and Data Beast settled down to dinner.

"Your mum calls Data Beast 'My lovely'," I laughed.

"Mum is pretty cool with Data Beast," said Roz. "Now, about that bat thief."

We looked at each other.

"How do you fancy getting some computer information on what is going on with the Supersave company?" I asked Data Beast.

Data Beast was picking some wires from his teeth.

"Find bad ones... yes?" he asked.

We nodded. He stood up and dived into the computer again.

Five seconds later, Data Beast was back.

"That was quick!" we both said.

"Firewall simple," the beast replied. "Nothing hidden from me. Money paid into bank far away. One hundred thousand pounds."

"Who was the money paid to?" asked Roz.

"Mrs... Price," answered Data Beast.

CHAPTER 4

Later that night, we arrived at an old lock-up at the edge of town. The place was a dump, but it had a brand new alarm system.

Data Beast was awesome. In a few seconds he disabled the alarm and opened the lock. We were in.

"Remember," whispered Roz, "we are looking for evidence of who is behind this bat business."

"But this is breaking and entering!"
I squeaked.

"Stop whining!" said Roz. "Can you
hear the bats?" she asked Data Beast.

Data Beast nodded. He pointed
his finger into the dark. I shone my
phone where he pointed. Suddenly he
made a rough clicking sound.

"Many of them... unhappy..."
he said.

Data Beast was right. There was a
stack of boxes against the far wall.

Roz ran over and looked between
the plastic slats.

"Oh, this is evil!" she whispered.

The boxes were full of bats. There
was no space for them to move.

Data Beast groaned. "So... sad. It hurts."

It was a strange moment. This monster Roz had made, caring about a bunch of bats. Roz smiled.

"You have a good heart, Data Beast," she said.

"What is... a heart?" asked Data Beast.

Roz didn't know what to say.

"She means that you're OK," I said.

The monster smiled a swirl of numbers.

"What next?" asked Roz.

"Revenge!" I replied.

36

CHAPTER 5

The Town Hall was packed. Most people wanted the new mall. But not everyone was keen. As we sat down, one of the developers was speaking.

"Our main concern is to bring jobs into the area!" he said.

"You must be kidding!" shouted a woman in the front row. "Your only concern is making money!"

"Please, ladies and gentlemen," said the Mayor. "If you wish to speak, put your hand up!"

Roz raised her hand.

"Now a question from a pupil from our local school," smiled the Mayor. "Isn't it great that you are getting a new classroom?"

Roz stood up.

"Yes, we get a new space, while the bats have their home nicked!" she said.

The whole room went silent. I looked at Price as he clenched his fist.

"But the bats have left the barn!" said the Mayor.

This was my moment. I had a special glove on to protect my skin from scratches. I lifted up one of the boxes and reached into it.

"So what's this then?" I asked.

People gasped at the sight of the bat. Data Beast was hiding in my phone. He made it vibrate to calm the bat down. Its ears stuck up, but it didn't move from my hand.

"The thing is," said Roz pointing at Mr Price, "our teacher moved the whole roost of bats and locked them in these boxes. That is a crime."

"It's all lies!" shouted Price. "That bat could have come from anywhere!"

"Really? What about the £100k in your wife's name, sitting in a secret bank account?" asked Roz. She held up a print-out as proof.

Price tried to make a run for it, but there were plenty of people in the hall who made sure he didn't get very far.

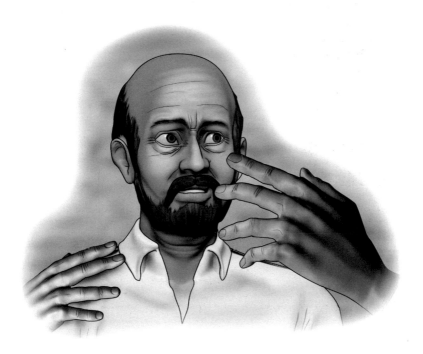

The next evening, we were down
by the old barn. The fence had gone.
The long-eared bats were flying round
our heads and catching insects.

"What happened to the
developers?" I asked Roz.

"Well, the plan to build the mall won't go ahead," she said. "And the guy who bribed Price has been caught. I don't think the head teacher was involved, but he wasn't pleased with me. He said that hacking was dangerous and illegal."

"Even if it's to uncover a crime?"
I asked. "Adults are messed up, aren't
they?"

"Some of them are," said Roz.
"Anyhow, the wood is safe for now.
It's a result."

I turned to the shadow at our side.

"You're a star, Data Beast!" I said.

"Star? I am?" asked Data Beast. He crouched down.

"Baby safe now," he said. In his hand, he held a young bat. He gently stroked its furry back. Then the bat gave a click, spread its wings and flew off to join the other bats.

47

FOR TEACHERS

About
Freestylers

Freestylers is a series of carefully levelled stories, especially geared for struggling readers of both sexes. With very low reading age and high interest age, these books are humorous, fun, up-to-the-minute and edgy. Core characters provide familiarity in all of the stories, build confidence and ease pupils from one story through to the next, accelerating reading progress.

Freestylers can be used for both guided and independent reading. To make the most of the books you can:

• Focus on making each reading session successful. Talk about the text before the pupil starts reading. Introduce the characters, the storyline and any unfamiliar vocabulary.

• Encourage the pupil to talk about the book during reading and after reading. How would they have felt if they were Roz? Or Kiran? How would they have reacted to the threat to the bat habitat?

• Talk about which parts of the story they like best and why.

For guidance, this story has been approximately measured to:

National Curriculum Level: 2A
Reading Age: 8.6
Book Band: White

ATOS: 3.3
Lexile ® Measure [confirmed]: 460L

BATS!

3 8002 02178 646 4

First published in 2014 by Wayland

Text copyright © Andrew Fusek Peters
Illustrations by Alex McArdell © Wayland

Wayland
338 Euston Road
London NW1 3BH

Wayland Australia
Level 17/207 Kent Street
Sydney, NSW 2000

The rights of Andrew Fusek Peters to be identified as the author
and Alex McArdell to be identified as the illustrator of this Work
have been asserted by them in accordance with the Copyright,
Designs and Patents Act, 1988.

All rights reserved

Consultant: Dee Reid
Editor: Nicola Edwards
Designer: Alyssa Peacock

A CIP catalogue record for this book is available from
the British Library.

Bats!. – (Freestylers data beast; 1)
823.9'2-dc23

ISBN: 978 0 7502 8231 4
E-book ISBN:978 0 7502 8812 5

Printed in China

Wayla	**Coventry City Council**	
	FML	
	3 8002 02178 646 4	
	Askews & Holts	Aug-2014
		£5.99